"I wasn't even on the porch—" Timothy began.

But his father interrupted him. "Timothy, don't argue with me! I *saw* you! And as soon as you heard me call you, you jumped up and ran into the woods."

Timothy shook his head desperately. "No! No! That wasn't me! It was—some kid who looks like me. Some kid—who stole my cap."

"Oh, come on, Timothy!" said his mother. "Some kid who looks like you?"

Can the T.C.D.C. solve this mystery and get Timothy out of trouble?

THE MYSTERY OF THE

DOUBLE TROUBLE

Elspeth Campbell Murphy
Illustrated by Chris Wold Dyrud

Chariot Books
David C. Cook Publishing Co.

A Wise Owl Book
Published by Chariot Books,
an imprint of David C. Cook Publishing Co.
David C. Cook Publishing Co., Elgin, Illinois 60120
David C. Cook Publishing Co., Weston, Ontario

The Mystery of the Double Trouble
© 1988 by Elspeth Campbell Murphy for text and Chris Wold
Dyrud for illustrations

Cover design by Chris Patchel
First Printing, 1988
Printed in the United States of America
93 92 91 90 89 88 5 4 3 2

Library of Congress Cataloging-in-Publication Data
Murphy, Elspeth Campbell.
    The mystery of the double trouble / Elspeth Campbell Murphy;
illustrated by Chris Wold Dyrud.
    p.   cm. — (The Ten commandments mysteries)
    Summary: Tim and his two cousins set out to find the boy who
seems to be his double and learn the meaning of the commandment
"Honor your father and your mother."
    ISBN 1-55513-545-5
    [1. Ten commandments—Fiction. 2. Cousins—Fiction. 3.
Mystery and detective stories.] I. Dyrud, Chris Wold, ill. II. Title.
III. Series: Murphy, Elspeth Campbell. Ten commandments
mysteries.
PZ7.M95316Myb   1988
[Fic]—dc19   87-26461
                                                             CIP
                                                             AC

"Honor your father and your mother."

Exodus 20:12 (NIV)

CONTENTS

1
BOYS AND GIRLS

The three cousins, Timothy Dawson, Titus Mc-
Kay, and Sarah-Jane Cooper, sat on the back
porch of Sarah-Jane's cabin at Misty Pines
Campground. They were all busy with different
things.

Timothy was busy pinning buttons on his baseball cap. He had way more buttons in his collection than he could fit on his cap at any one time.
So, once in a while, he took off all the old
buttons, and he stuck on new ones. He was pretty
fussy about it. Timothy was nice about sharing
his stuff, but he never let anyone wear his cap.

Titus was busy trying to tear open a packet of
chocolate-covered marshmallow cookies with his
teeth.

Sarah-Jane was busy studying the baby clothes

in a big, fat catalog and turning down the corners of the pages. She said, "I almost have all my furniture picked out for when I get married. Next I have to pick out baby clothes. Do you want to help me?"

"No, thanks," said Timothy, without looking up from his buttons.

"Mrumph," said Titus.

Sarah-Jane went on. "I saw this picture in the paper of quintuplets—that's five babies all born at the same time. It's like twins, only there are five instead of two."

"I know," said Timothy.

"Mrumph," said Titus.

Sarah-Jane went on. "Those little quints looked so sweet and cute and cuddly, all lying in a row. So I decided that's what I'm going to do— have quintuplets. I'll have the five, sweetest little babies you ever saw—four girls and one boy. Do you want to hear the names I picked out?"

"No," said Timothy and Titus together.

"OK," said Sarah-Jane. "Here they are, in alphabetical order: Alison, Bonita, Cynthia, Daniel, and Danielle. Now, do you want to hear

10

the nicknames?''

"NO!" said Timothy and Titus together.

"OK," said Sarah-Jane. "Here they are, in alphabetical order: Ali, Bonnie, Cindy, Danny, and Dani."

"That's crazy!" said Titus, finally getting the cookie packet open. "You'll have two kids with the same name."

"No, I won't," said Sarah-Jane. "The *boy* is Danny with a *y*, and the *girl* is Dani with an *i*."

Timothy looked up from his buttons long enough to help himself to a cookie. "But it's still crazy, S-J," he pointed out. "You can't *see* how the names are spelled when you just say them. So you'll still have two kids with the same name."

"No, I won't," said Sarah-Jane. "Because they'll always wear cute little clothes with their names sewn on the front and back."

"Oh, brother," groaned Titus. But it came out "Mo-bruffah," because he was starting on his third cookie.

Sarah-Jane ignored him and went right on talking. "I'll always dress them all alike. And they'll be so good. They won't even cry that much,

11

except maybe a little bit when they're hungry or scared and they want their mother, which is me, of course.

"And I'll teach them the commandment that says, 'Honor your father and your mother.' I'll do that right away—as soon as they're born—before they can even *think* about acting up. And what will they have to complain about, anyway? Because I'll never make them eat broccoli. And they'll have lots of baby toys and all these cute little basinettes lined up in a row and cute little clothes . . . "

Titus interrupted, "Have a cookie, S-J. *Please*!"

"Boys! Ha! What do they know?" said Sarah-Jane, taking a cookie anyway. "If there were another girl around here, she'd look at the catalog with me, and we could think up baby names together."

But the problem was, there weren't any kids the right age at Misty Pines this year. There were plenty of *kids*—if you didn't mind four year olds—but Sarah-Jane kept wishing for a girl her own age.

2
OFF LIMITS

The boys had been visiting at the Coopers' cabin all week, while Sarah-Jane's parents helped to build the Wayfarer's Chapel. But now Timothy's and Titus's parents had come up to spend a couple of days and then take the boys back with them.

Sarah-Jane kept checking the other cabins and the lodge for new kids, saying she didn't know who in the world she was supposed to play with after Tim and Ti left.

Just then the kids' moms came out on the porch.

Timothy's mother (Aunt Sarah) said, "As soon as Priscilla wakes up from her nap, we'll go to the Seven Rainbows Waterfall."

"Neat-O!" said Timothy.

"EXcellent!" said Titus.

Sarah-Jane said, "And can we still go on the moonlight boat trip on the *Queen-of-the-Lake* tonight?" The cousins had been on the daytime ride. But this time they would be up extralate and out after dark.

"Yes," said her mother. "If you three are on your best behavior today."

"What about Priscilla?" asked Timothy.

"Don't be silly, Timothy," said his mother. "Your sister is just a baby. But, speaking of Priscilla—I want you to put those buttons away.

14

If she puts one of them in her mouth, she could cut herself.''

"But I'm not done with my cap yet," protested Timothy.

"You can finish it when we get back from Seven Rainbows," said his mother. "I don't want any loose buttons lying around."

Reluctantly, Timothy closed the old fishing tackle box he used for his buttons, and snapped it shut. That way, his baby sister couldn't get into it.

"Speaking of putting things in your mouth," said Titus's mother (Aunt Jane). "What are you kids eating?"

Quickly Titus shoved the packet of cookies behind his back. "Mom, you *said* we could go to that little grocery store. You *said*! And I bought these cookies with my own spending money. I even shared them with Tim and S-J!"

"That's fine," said his mother. "But I think I'd better look after them for you."

"That's not fair!" Titus howled. "I bought them with my own money. So I should be allowed to look after them myself!"

"Titus," said his mother. "I have seen how you get when you're around chocolate-covered marshmallow cookies. You eat one right after another. You can't stop yourself. Then, before you know it, you're sick to your stomach. Now, hand it over."

Titus looked like he wanted to argue some more. But Timothy muttered out of the corner of his mouth, "Come on, Ti! Don't blow the boat trip."

Reluctantly, Titus handed over the bag. It was almost half empty already. "How many of these did you eat?" asked his mother.

Titus held up a cookie that he hadn't taken a bite out of yet. "This is only my fourth," he said.

Without a word, his mother opened the bag and made him drop that one in.

"Aw, Mom!" said Titus.

"Don't 'aw, Mom,' me," said his mother. "You can come ask me when you want one later. Much later. Believe me. This is for your own good." She slipped the bag of cookies into her tote bag. Titus could see them as plain as anything sticking over the top, but he knew they were still *Off Limits*.

Timothy gave his mother the button box, so that Titus wouldn't be the only one handing something over.

"Look how brown Timothy got over the summer!" said Sarah-Jane's mother (Aunt Sue). "And his hair got so bleached by the sun! That bright, blue T-shirt you got from Indian Trails souvenir shop looks very nice on you, Timothy."

"Thank you," said Timothy. "As soon as I get my cap finished, I'll be all set."

"Mom, may I borrow your scissors?" asked Sarah-Jane, pulling them out of her mother's needlework basket.

"What for?" asked her mother.

"I want to cut baby clothes out of the catalog."

"Oh, no, you don't! I brought that catalog up here to look at on vacation. But I haven't even had a chance to see it yet."

"But I need to cut out baby clothes for my quintuplets, Ali, Bonnie, Cindy, Danny, and Dani," protested Sarah-Jane.

"You can *look* at it all you want to," said her mother. "But don't cut up a thing until I tell you

I'm all done with it."

Reluctantly, Sarah-Jane set the scissors and catalog aside.

Just at that moment Priscilla yelled her little baby head off to let everyone know that naptime was *over*.

As Aunt Sarah and Sarah-Jane went to get her, Aunt Sarah said with a laugh, "Are you sure you want *quintuplets*?"

3
WHO'S TONY?

When they got back from the Seven Rainbows Waterfall later that afternoon, the cousins went straight to the playground behind the lodge.

They couldn't stop talking about the moonlight boat trip on the *Queen-of-the-Lake*. They couldn't decide if it made the time go faster to talk about it—or to forget about it.

While they were climbing on the monkey bars, a man and a lady came around the side of the lodge. They smiled and waved to the cousins from a distance.

"Who's that?" asked Titus.

"Never saw them before in my life," said Timothy.

"They're probably some friends of my mom and dad's," said Sarah-Jane.

So—just to be polite—the cousins smiled and waved back.

The couple seemed happy as they turned and went inside.

The cousins played for a while longer. Then Titus and Sarah-Jane had to go to the bathroom. Sarah-Jane knew where the bathrooms were in the lodge, and it was a lot closer than going back to the cabin. So they left Timothy playing on the slide and said they would be right back.

Sarah-Jane showed Titus the little hallway off the lobby where the men's and women's rooms were.

They met again in the lobby. They were on their way down the front steps when suddenly the lady they had seen earlier hurried up to them.

All in a rush she said, "Oh, you're Tony's new friends! Listen, I hate to rush off, but Tony's dad and I just remembered a couple of things we need to get in town. I left a note at the desk. But you can tell Tony yourselves, too. We'll be gone only about an hour or so. Oops! Here's my husband with the car. Bye, bye! Talk to you later!"

The lady had talked so fast, Titus and Sarah-

Jane hadn't been able to get a word in edgewise.

They watched the car drive off. Then they turned to each other and said, *"Who's Tony??"*

4
WHERE'S TIM?

When Sarah-Jane and Titus got back to the playground, Timothy was gone.

Then they spotted his bright blue, Indian Trails T-shirt beyond the trees at the edge of the playground.

Titus said, "Look. Tim's wearing his cap now. He must have gone back to the cabin to get it."

"But he wasn't finished putting the buttons on it," said Sarah-Jane. "You know how fussy he is. He never wears his cap until he gets the buttons exactly the way he wants them."

Just then Timothy joined them. But he didn't come from the direction of the woods behind the lodge. He came from the direction of the lake in front of the lodge. He was bareheaded, and the sun shone on his bright, blond hair.

"Tim!" cried Titus. "Where did you just come from?"

"From the lake," said Timothy in surprise. "I went to see if the water is warm enough for swimming. Why are you guys looking at me so funny?"

"Because—but—but you were in the woods a couple of minutes ago!" Titus spluttered.

All three of them looked toward the woods. There was no one there.

"I don't get it," said Titus. "How did you get up to the woods, down to the lake, and back to the playground so fast?''

"I wasn't *in* the woods," said Timothy. "I never went there at all."

"But we *saw* you!" cried Titus. "You were wearing your button cap and everything—" He stopped suddenly. "Where's your cap? Why aren't you wearing it now?"

Timothy looked at Titus as if his cousin were going crazy. "I wasn't wearing my cap. I *couldn't* have been wearing it, because I wasn't finished putting the buttons on it yet."

"That's what *I* said," put in Sarah-Jane.

"OK," said Titus, taking a deep breath. " But *somebody* was wearing a button cap. Somebody who looks exactly like Tim."

"WHAT?!" cried Timothy. "This is crazy! There aren't even any kids our age around here. You must be imagining things!"

"*Both* of us?" asked Titus. "S-J and I both saw you—or somebody. Right, S-J?"

Sarah-Jane nodded vigorously.

"OK," said Timothy. "Let's get to the bottom of this. Let's go back to the cabin, and I'll show you my cap. That will *prove* I wasn't wearing it in the woods just now.''

"OK,'' said Titus. ''But what if your cap isn't there?''

"What if somebody *stole* it?'' asked Sarah-Jane.

"It'd better not be stolen!'' cried Timothy. ''Because whoever took it is going to be in big trouble!''

But when the three cousins got to the cabin, they found out that *they* were the ones in trouble.

Big, big trouble.

5
BIG TROUBLE

Their parents were on the back porch—waiting for them.

Sarah-Jane got yelled at first.

"What did I tell you about the catalog, Sarah-Jane?" asked her mother. "Didn't I specifically say, 'Do *not* cut up the catalog before I've had a chance to see it'?"

"But I *didn't*!" exclaimed Sarah-Jane.

"Then what do you call *this?*" asked her mother. She held up the catalog and scissors. Scraps of paper hung from the catalog where some pictures of baby furniture had been carefully snipped out.

"But—but—I didn't do that!" cried Sarah-Jane.

But they didn't have time to talk about it,

because now it was Titus's turn to get yelled at.

His mother held up the cookie packet. There were only two cookies left, plus some crumbs. "And what about these cookies, Titus? Or what's left of them? I told you that you had to ask me before you could have anymore."

"But I *didn't*!" exclaimed Titus. "I mean, I didn't take any. I didn't even come back to the cabin. You can ask S-J. I was with her the whole time."

But they didn't have time to talk about it, because now it was Timothy's turn to get yelled at.

His mother said, "We have a rule about that button collection of yours, Timothy. You can't leave any loose buttons lying around, because Priscilla might get them."

Timothy's mouth dropped open in surprise when he looked at the spot on the porch where his mother was pointing. His tackle box was sitting open, and some of his best buttons were arranged by color and size on the porch floor. His cap was nowhere to be seen.

"Who was messing with my stuff?" Timothy

cried.

But they didn't have time to talk about it, because just then Timothy's dad stepped out onto the porch. He looked pretty mad.

Titus and Sarah-Jane were in trouble. But Timothy was in *double* trouble.

"And another thing, Timothy!" said his father. "Your mother and I have had a rule for you ever since you were a toddler. What are you supposed to do when one of us calls you?"

"I'm supposed to come when I'm called," replied Timothy, surprised that his father would even ask him about such a simple rule.

"Then why didn't you?" demanded his father. "Why did you just run off like that?"

"When?" asked Timothy, sounding more puzzled than ever. "I never heard you calling me."

"What do you mean you didn't hear me? You were playing right here on the porch! I was going to fix the kitchen faucet, and I called to you to get my toolbox out of the car."

"I wasn't even on the porch—" Timothy began. "I was—"

But his father interrupted him. "Timothy, don't argue with me! I *saw* you! And as soon as you heard me call you, you jumped up and ran into the woods. I called after you, but you just ran faster."

Timothy shook his head desperately. "No! No! That wasn't me! It was—it was—some kid who looks like me. Some kid—who stole my cap."

"Oh, come on, Timothy!" said his mother. "Some kid who looks like you? Some kid who stole your cap? Next I suppose you're going to say that this mystery child left your buttons all over the place."

"That's exactly right, Aunt Sarah!" exclaimed Sarah-Jane, answering for Timothy, who couldn't get his words out. "And I bet it was the same person who cut up my catalog and ate Ti's cookies!"

Aunt Jane sighed. "Do you know what this reminds me of? When Titus was about three years old, he had an imaginary playmate called Sam. Every time Titus did something wrong, Sam got blamed for it.

"*Sam* was the one who poured cooking oil on the kitchen floor and went 'skating.' *Sam* was the one who made boats out of mother's best stationery and floated them in the bathtub. *Sam* was the one who hid his lima beans in Titus's pockets."

Even though they were all in big trouble, Timothy and Sarah-Jane couldn't help giggling.

Timothy said, "Wow, Ti! You were really *bad*!"

Sarah-Jane said, "Yeah! My quintuplets better never act like that!"

But the grown-ups didn't think things were so funny.

Titus's mother pointed to the cut-up catalog,

the almost-empty cookie packet, and the lined-up buttons. She said in a disbelieving voice, "So what are you kids saying? That 'Sam' did all this?"

"No," said Titus seriously. "It was some boy called Tony."

6
TIM'S DOUBLE

The grown-ups and Timothy all asked the same question that Titus and Sarah-Jane had asked earlier: *"Who's Tony?"*

Titus explained. "This man and lady waved to us from the lodge when we were out on the playground. We thought they were just being friendly, so we waved back. Then later, the lady said to S-J and me, 'Oh, you're Tony's new friends.' Well, S-J and I weren't playing with anybody called Tony. We were just playing with Tim. But maybe the lady *thought Tim was Tony.* And maybe Uncle Paul *thought Tony was Tim.*"

The grown-ups all looked at one another as if they didn't know what to think.

At last Timothy's father said, "We don't want to be unfair to you guys. But this is serious business. You know what the commandment says—'Honor your father and your mother.' It's bad enough to disobey us, but it's even worse to lie about it.''

''But we're *not* lying!'' said Timothy earnestly.

''And we didn't even mess up in the first place!'' said Sarah-Jane. Then she added in a small voice, ''Are we still going on the *Queen-of-the-Lake* tonight?'' (She knew it was probably the wrong time to ask, but she had to know.)

''We parents need to talk all this over,'' said her mother. ''We have to decide whether to ground you—or whether to believe this far-fetched story about Timothy's double.''

''What's a double?'' asked Titus.

''It's someone who looks exactly like someone else,'' said his mother.

''You mean like twins—or quints?'' Sarah-Jane asked.

''Yes,'' said her aunt. ''Except a double isn't in the same family. They say a person's double is a stranger who looks exactly like him.''

''Can that really happen?'' asked Sarah-Jane.

"No," said her Aunt Jane. "Because God didn't make any two people exactly alike—not even identical twins. But sometimes two strangers can look a lot like each other, especially from a distance."

"The way Tony looks like Tim," said Titus.

His mother sighed. "If there even *is* a Tony. If he's not just someone you imagined."

"We didn't imagine him," said Titus firmly. "There's some boy running around who looks like Tim's double."

"Yeah," said Timothy. "And this *double* is causing me *trouble*!"

7
THE CHASE

"How can we make them believe us?" Sarah-Jane asked her cousins when the grown-ups had gone inside the cabin.

"What we need is *proof*!" said Titus.

"Then what are we waiting for?" asked Timothy. "We're detectives, aren't we? So let's go find this kid Tony."

They decided to start looking in the woods, since that's where Uncle Paul, Titus, and Sarah-Jane had all spotted the fake Tim.

They had gone only a short way when Timothy suddenly cried, "Aha!"

"What—what—what?" asked Sarah-Jane and Titus. "What did you find? A clue?"

"Sure did!" said Timothy triumphantly. "Look at this!"

He held out a red, white, and blue button that said, *I Like Ike*.

"Who's Ike?" asked Titus.

"He was some president a long time ago," said Timothy. "My neighbor gave me this button when she cleaned out her basement."

"You mean this is *your* button?" asked Titus. "You think it fell off your hat?"

"That's exactly what I think," said Timothy. "It probably wasn't pinned on all the way."

Sarah-Jane said, "That means that Tony came by here. Let's keep looking."

They decided to walk in the woods along the edge of the field. And they decided to walk in the direction of the lodge, since that's where Tony's parents were staying.

They walked in a single file. Timothy went first, followed by Titus and Sarah-Jane. They tried to look around for Tony and look at the ground for more clues at the same time. It wasn't easy.

Suddenly Timothy came to a dead stop, causing Titus and Sarah-Jane to tumble into him.

"It's so weird!" breathed Timothy. "Look!"

He pointed to a solitary figure far ahead of them.

Titus and Sarah-Jane looked, but they could hardly believe their eyes. They saw a kid with long, tanned arms and legs—like Timothy. He was wearing a bright blue, Indian Trails T-shirt—like Timothy. And his hair was white-blond—what they could see of it peeking out from under Timothy's baseball cap.

Quickly Titus and Sarah-Jane turned back to Timothy, as if to make sure he was still there with them.

Then Sarah-Jane roused herself as if she were

waking up from a dream. "Come on," she said briskly. "Tony's getting away."

They hurried after him, trying to be super-quiet. But Tony must have had good ears, because he suddenly turned and saw them coming after him.

Tony took off, running like the wind. He raced out of the woods, past the playground, around the front of the lodge, and up the steps—with Timothy, Titus, and Sarah-Jane charging after him.

The three cousins burst through the front door just in time to see Tony disappear into the little, dead-end hallway where the bathrooms were.

"Ha!" panted Timothy. "We've got you cornered, Double Trouble! And you have a lot of explaining to do!"

He and Titus marched triumphantly into the men's room.

There was no one there.

8
THE CAPTURE

Slowly the boys came out into the hallway where Sarah-Jane was waiting for them.

"Well?" she asked.

"Nothing," said Timothy in disbelief. "He's not in there. And there's no window he could have climbed out of. How did he get out without us seeing him? I'm beginning to think I'm imagining things after all!"

Sarah-Jane said, "I've been here in the hallway the whole time, and no one came past me."

Timothy said, "That means he must have gone into the other bathroom."

Sarah-Jane was absolutely shocked. "You mean a *boy* went into the *girls'* bathroom?! I'm telling!"

Titus said, "No—no, wait a minute, S-J! May-

be a *boy* didn't go into the ladies' room. Maybe a *girl* did!''

"WHAT?!" said Timothy and Sarah-Jane together.

"It's like your quints, S-J!" said Titus. "You know, the ones with the same name—Danny with a *y* and Dani with an *i*. Well, it's the same way with the name Tony, isn't it? I mean, if you spell it with a *y*, it's a boy's name. But if you spell it with an *i*, it's a girl's name. We just assumed Tony was a boy, because he—I mean, she—looks like Tim."

"I don't look like a girl!" objected Timothy.

"No, of course, not," said Titus quickly. "But girls can have short blonde hair and blue T-shirts, too. I think *Tony* is really *Toni*. And I think she's hiding in the ladies' bathroom."

Timothy and Sarah-Jane nodded. They just knew he was right.

Sarah-Jane said, "Stand back, gentlemen. This is a job for a *lady*."

She swept grandly into the women's bathroom and hollered, "All right, Toni-with-an-i! You come out of there right this minute, do you hear me? You have a lot of explaining to do, girl!"

Toni-with-an-i gave up and came slowly out into the hallway.

9
THE EXPLANATION

It was amazing.

Toni (which they found out was short for Antonia) looked more like Timothy than Sarah-Jane or Titus did—and she wasn't even related! Toni definitely looked like a girl, and Timothy definitely looked like a boy. But they looked enough alike to be brother and sister.

"So what's the story, Antonia?" demanded Sarah-Jane. "Why did you get us into so much trouble?"

"I didn't mean to!" said Toni. "You've got to believe me! See, I didn't want to come up here to Misty Pines in the first place—because I was afraid there wouldn't be any kids to play with. And I was mad at my mother because she wouldn't buy me all the stuff I wanted at Indian

Trails—just this T-shirt.

"So when we got here, I decided I'd show them. I wasn't going to go far. I just thought I'd hide out and make them think I was lost. So anyway. I was walking behind the cabins, and I saw your stuff on the porch. And I knew kids must live there. "But you weren't home."

"We were at the Seven Rainbows Waterfall," said Sarah-Jane.

Toni nodded. "Well, I didn't know where you were or when you'd be back. And I had to keep away from the lodge and the playground in case my parents saw me. I didn't think you'd mind if I sort of played with your stuff. I was just going to wait around. But when someone's dad called me *Timothy*, I didn't know what to do. So I figured I'd better get out of there fast.

"I didn't even stop to take off the button cap. And I ran into the woods. But then, when I saw you coming back to the cabin, I doubled back. And—and—I overheard you all get yelled at."

Titus was indignant. "What? You heard? Then why didn't you step out and *prove* we weren't making up some farfetched story about Tim having a double?"

"I was afraid everyone would be mad at me," said Toni.

"Well, yeah, we would have been," admitted Titus.

"I didn't really mean to get you in trouble," Toni said again. "The cap was so neat, I thought I'd just try it on. And I thought you were going to cut up the catalog anyway, because I saw the scissors lying there with it. I love catalogs! And I was getting pretty hungry, so I ate some cookies. I didn't know they were off limits."

"Well, now you can come back with us to the cabin and get us out of trouble with our parents," said Sarah-Jane.

"Parents!" cried Toni. "Oh, no! I forgot all about *my* parents! They still think I'm lost! I bet they've called out the forest rangers by now. I'm going to have to hide for the rest of my life!"

THE T.C.D.C.

But there was nowhere to hide, because who should be strolling by the cabin when the kids got there but Toni's parents.

Toni's parents and the cousins' parents all stared at Timothy and Toni, as if they couldn't understand what they were seeing.

It took a *long time* for the kids to explain everything. The cousins' parents said they were sorry for blaming their kids for something they didn't do. And the cousins said, "That's OK."

Toni asked her parents, "Are you still mad at me for running away?"

Her mother said, "Of course we're mad that you did such a crazy thing! Except—um—we didn't know you were gone."

"WHAT?!" cried Toni.

"Well, we thought it was *you* we saw on the playground with Titus and Sarah-Jane. We were just so happy that you'd found some new friends already."

But Toni said, "You mean I went to all that trouble for nothing?"

"Toni! Think of all the trouble you *caused*—for Timothy, Titus, and Sarah-Jane!" said her parents.

"Yeah!" said Timothy.

Titus said, "It's just a good thing the T.C.D.C. could handle it."

"What's a 'teesy-deesy'?" asked Toni.

"It's letters," explained Sarah-Jane.
"Capital T.
Capital C.
Capital D.
Capital C.
It stands for the Three Cousins Detective Club."

"Can anyone join?" asked Toni wistfully. "Or do you have to be a cousin?"

"You have to be a cousin," said Sarah-Jane. "But you can play with us if you want to. And maybe you can even go on the *Queen-of-the-Lake* boat trip with us tonight.''

But Toni's father said, "No boat trip for Toni, I'm afraid. She has to be grounded for a while to think about not running away and not messing with other people's property. But she can play with you kids tomorrow.''

Toni said to the cousins, "I'll see you guys tomorrow, OK? And I promise—no more *double trouble*!''

The End